Cars

The first motorcars were made in Europe over 100 years ago. They looked a lot like the horse-drawn carriages that were commonly used at the the time. Today, they come in all sorts of shapes and sizes for use in many different places.

City Car

City cars are perfect for driving on busy city streets. Plastic body panels make them very light, meaning they use less fuel when on the move. Their small size also makes it easier to fit into tight parking spaces.

DISCOVERY FACT™

There are more than 1 billion cars in use around the world.

Jet Airliner

Jet airliners are the largest passenger aircraft and the biggest can carry around 525 passengers. Despite their massive size and weight, they are still able to reach speeds of over 560 miles per hour, using powerful jet engines.

Chinook

Chinook helicopters have double propellers and are able to lift heavy objects. They are often used to carry vehicles, such as jeeps, small boats, and even fighter jets, into hard-to-reach places.

Jet Fighter

Jet fighters are fast and can change direction in the air very quickly. Some models can fly at three times the speed of sound. That's the same as over 1,800 miles per hour at ground level. That's about the same as going across the whole of North America in under 2 hours.

Sea Plane

Sea planes are designed to take off and land on water, instead of using a runway. These aircraft have two floats underneath instead of wheels, which act like a giant water ski.

Sports Car

Sports cars have bodies that are shaped to help them go fast and they have more powerful engines than regular road cars. Sports cars are often painted in bright colors to stand out.

SUV

SUV stands for Sports Utility Vehicle. SUVs have chunky tyres for better control over off-road ground. The engine powers all four wheels of an SUV. This is called four-wheel drive and it helps the SUV to keep moving, even through mud and over rocks.

Racing Car

The front and rear wings on a racing car push the wheels down onto the surface of the track. This means they can go around corners much faster than other cars. Every part of a racing car is made for high performance to help the car win races.

Classic Car

Classic cars may not be as fast or as safe as modern cars, but many people still like to collect them for their beautiful designs and unusual features. Owners will often enter their cars into competitions at special meetings, called vintage rallies.

Chopper

Choppers are motorcycles made using the chopped-up pieces of other cycles. Popular features include extra-long front forks with lots of shiny metal, called chrome, on the bodywork.

The Honda Cub is the most popular motorcycle ever. Over 60 million have been made since 1958.

The top
called Moto
reach spee
per hour. D
lean their bik
the ground in order t
corners as fast as possible.

Motorcycles

In many parts of the world, motorcycles are the main form of transportation. In India and many parts of Asia, they are much more popular than cars. Motorcycles are used throughout the world for leisure activities such as road-trips or racing.

Supercar

Supercars are the fastest and most expensive cars on the road. They can accelerate to 60 miles per hour in under 3 seconds and reach top speeds of over 250 miles per hour!

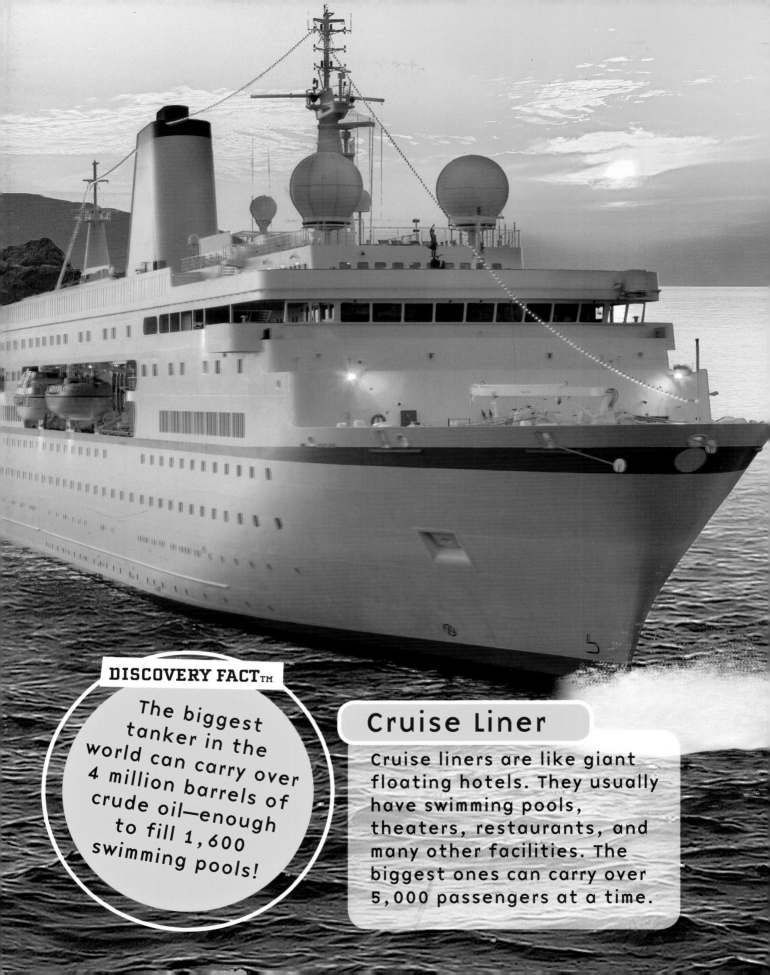

The biggest tanker in the world can carry over 4 million barrels of crude oil—enough to fill 1,600 swimming pools!

Cruise Liner

Cruise liners are like giant floating hotels. They usually have swimming pools, theaters, restaurants, and many other facilities. The biggest ones can carry over 5,000 passengers at a time.

Shock absorbers

Motocross Cycle

Motocross cycles are designed for using off-road. The knobbly tires on a motocross cycle keep them from slipping on muddy dirt tracks. Extra-large shock absorbers cushion the rider's landing when going over bumps and jumps.

Scooter

Scooters are the smallest model of motorcycle and are designed to be easy to get about through traffic on busy city streets. Their small engines mean that they do not use very much fuel.

Sport Cycle

Sport cycles are designed to be fast and fun to ride. Sport cycles have big engines and lightweight materials to help them accelerate. Wide tires give sport cycles more grip on the road and special brakes help the rider slow down.

Boats

For a long time before the invention of railroads and cars, it was actually easier for people to travel by river and sea than over land. The first simpl__ __oats were made from carved-out tree ___ __ry different to the many, varied b____ ___ ___day.

Hovercraft

Hovercrafts are amazing vehicles that can travel across both land and water. A cushion of air is pushed down into an inflatable fabric skirt at the bottom. This allows the body of the craft to hover above the surface. When a hovercraft moves it is actually flying, and is steered by a pilot.

Hybrid

Hybrid vehicles have both a regular engine and an electric motor. Hybrids use electric power when driving at low speeds, saving fuel and therefore giving out less pollution.

Cars are currently being developed that can drive themselves, using cameras and computers to steer and avoid accidents.

Truck-mounted Crane

Truck-mounted cranes are able to travel easily from one site to another. The crane arm fits inside itself like a telescope while on the move. At the site, heavy metal legs extend out from the base of the truck to keep it stable. The crane arm then extends upward, ready to lift things.

The name "bulldozer" comes from an old American expression, meaning to push or shove something.

Bulldozer

Bulldozers have a large metal blade at the front, designed to push sand, rubble, and other materials around the construction site. Giant wheels give them better grip when moving over soft and uneven ground because they spread the weight.

Concrete Mixer

Concrete mixers are used to deliver concrete to the construction site. The mixing drum on the back keeps turning, meaning the concrete does not set, and can be poured where it is needed before it goes hard.

Dump Truck

Dump trucks are designed for moving heavy materials to and from the construction site. Extra-strong suspension is needed to support the weight of the load, while over-sized tires cushion the ride over rough ground.

Tanker

Tankers are the largest ships on the sea. They are used to transport massive quantities of oil and other cargo around the globe. The biggest tanker ever built would be taller than the Empire State Building if it was stood upright!

Power Boat

Power boats are specially made for high-speed racing. When they accelerate, the front of the boat lifts up out of the water, allowing them to reach high speeds as they skim across the surface.

Catamaran

The bottom of a boat is called a hull. A catamaran has two hulls with a gap in between. This design lowers the amount of the boat which drags through the water, meaning it can move more quickly and smoothly over the surface.

Jet Ski

Jet skis are light, easy to move, and fast. They are used for fun and for racing, as well as competitions, where riders compete to do the best tricks and jumps.

Construction Vehicles

Construction vehicles have heavy-duty bodywork, powerful engines, and lots of special tools designed to help builders with their work on-site. They are painted bright colors, such as yellow or red, for extra safety, as this makes them easier to see.

The world's tallest truck-mounted crane extends to 330 feet in height.

Excavator

Excavators are used for digging out trenches and foundations for buildings. The cab, hydraulic arm, and bucket are able to turn a full circle. This allows the driver to move earth and building materials in every direction.

Road Roller

Road rollers are used to compact earth, gravel, and asphalt when making a new road. The heavy metal drum acts like a rolling pin on pastry, pressing down on the freshly laid surface to make it smooth and solid.

Vehicles of the Future

The vehicles of the future will need to use less fuel and make less pollution. Scientists are currently developing new ways to make traveling cleaner, cheaper, and better for the environment. Which of these vehicles will you be driving in the future?

Concept Car

Concept cars are a way for motor companies to show off their new ideas for the future. This one is a very light electric vehicle with one seat. It's designed to be used for short journeys and to take up less space on the road.

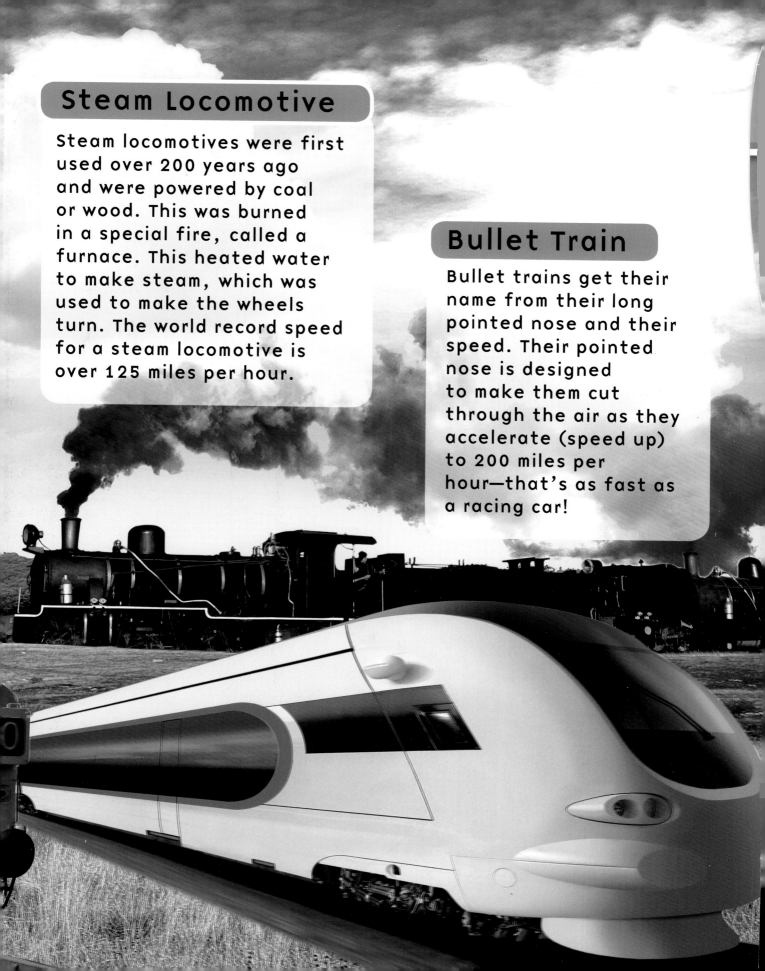

Steam Locomotive

Steam locomotives were first used over 200 years ago and were powered by coal or wood. This was burned in a special fire, called a furnace. This heated water to make steam, which was used to make the wheels turn. The world record speed for a steam locomotive is over 125 miles per hour.

Bullet Train

Bullet trains get their name from their long pointed nose and their speed. Their pointed nose is designed to make them cut through the air as they accelerate (speed up) to 200 miles per hour—that's as fast as a racing car!

Aircraft

Modern aircraft have developed a lot since the Wright brothers made the first-ever airplane flight in 1903. Today, powerful jet engines mean planes can carry hundreds of passengers long distances and fly faster than the speed of sound.

Stealth Plane

Stealth planes have special features to help keep them hidden from the enemy. Their unusual flat shape is hard for radar signals to pick up. The plane's engines are hidden inside the wings so that heat sensors can't see the heat they make.

DISCOVERY FACT™

The fastest aircraft in the world is the U.S. Military Falcon HTV-2. It reaches speeds of over 12,000 miles per hour and flies without a pilot.

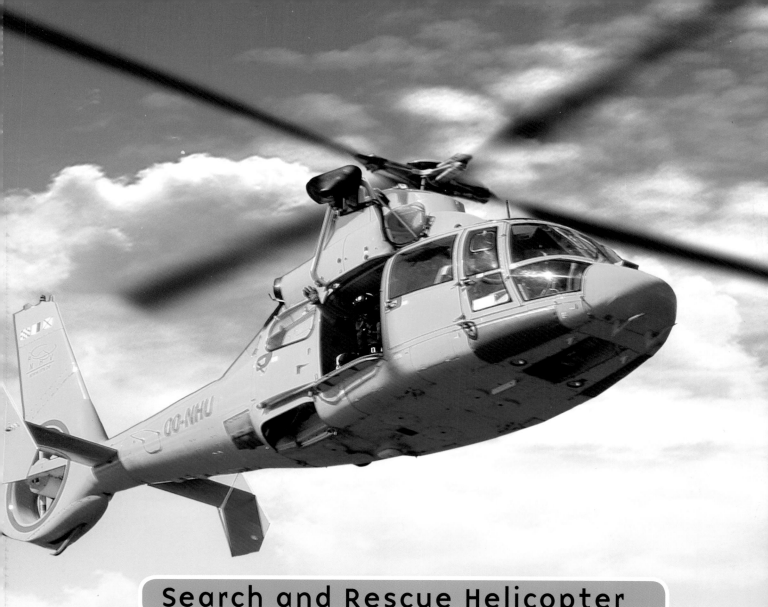

Search and Rescue Helicopter

Search and rescue helicopters often face difficult weather conditions and carry out hard tasks. They get to places where no other vehicle can reach, such as mountain ranges and rough seas. A special rope lowers to the ground so that people can be pulled up to safety without the helicopter having to land.

The longest rail tunnel in the world is the Gotthard Base Tunnel, which runs for 35 miles under the Swiss Alps in Europe.

Diesel Locomotive

Diesel locomotives are the most widely used engines on modern railroads. They can be used to pull passenger trains and cargo. The longest ever diesel-powered train had 682 carriages and was over 4.5 miles long!